How the BIRDS Got Their SONGS

Gaa-pi-onji Mino'amaazowaad Ingiweg Bebaamaashiwaad

To Josephine (Drouillard) Zimmerman and all our Zimmerman and Drouillard relatives. – TZ & SZ

With special acknowledgment to my children Tyler and Talisha and grandsons Theo and Thatcher. – TZ

With special acknowledgment to my parents, family, friends, and the Gichi-onigamiing / Grand Portage community. – SZ

How the BIRDS Got Their SONGS

Gaa-pi-onji Mino'amaazowaad Ingiweg Bebaamaashiwaad

STORY BY
TRAVIS ZIMMERMAN

ILLUSTRATIONS BY
**SAM ZIMMERMAN /
ZHAAWANOOGIIZHIK**

RETOLD IN OJIBWEMOWIN BY
**MARCUS AMMESMAKI /
AANIKANOOTAAGEWIN**

GAA-INAAJIMOD:
TRAVIS ZIMMERMAN

GAA-MAZINIBII'ANG:
**SAM ZIMMERMAN /
ZHAAWANOOGIIZHIK**

GAA-ANISHINAABEWISIDOOD:
**MARCUS AMMESMAKI /
AANIKANOOTAAGEWIN**

MINNESOTA
HISTORICAL
SOCIETY PRESS

When Mother Earth was very young and the Great Spirit had created all the beings—the two-legged, the four-legged, those that swim, those that fly, and those that crawl—he noticed how quiet everything was. As he walked about the earth, listening to the sounds of the animals and the wind and the waters, some birds flying by caught his eye. He knew immediately what he needed to do.

Weshkad imaa akina gegoo gaa-ozhitood awe Manidoo Naagaanizid, biinish igo ingiweg sa naazhoogaadewaad, naayogaadewaad, bebaamaashiwaad, naa ge wiinawaa bemoodewaad. Miish imaa gaa-izhi-maaminonendang awe Manidoo epiichi-bizhishigwaanig imaa. Mii go imaa akiikaang gaa-izhi-babaamosed baa-bizindawaad iniwen awesiinyan biinish igo niiwin wendaanimadinigin naa ge ezhijiwaninig iwe nibi. Miish imaa gaa-izhi-maaminonenimaad iniwen aanind bineshiinyan. Gaabige go naa gaa-izhi-gikendang ge-izhichigepan awe Manidoo Naagaanizid.

The next day the Great Spirit assembled all the birds and told them he was going to give each bird their own special song. All the birds were there, from the littlest of birds like the sparrows, thrushes, and chickadees...

Wayaabaninig idash ogii-asiginaan akina iniwen bineshiinyan gii-inaad igo ji-miinaad iniwen wiinawaa igo odinwewiniwaan. Aazha eni-maamawishkaawaad akina go naa ingiweg bineshiinyag, biinish igo ingiweg bineshiinsag, aanakoog, naa ge wiinawaa gijigaaneshiinyag...

… to the biggest and most powerful birds like the ravens, hawks, and the mighty eagle.

… biinish igo ge wiinawaa binesiwag daabishkoo ingiweg gaagaagiwag, gekekwag, naa ge ingiweg migiziwag.

The Great Spirit told the birds they should fly as high as they could toward the sun. When they could not fly any higher, they should turn around, and they would learn their song on their way back to Mother Earth. The higher they flew, the prettier their song would be.

Ogii-inaan awe Manidoo Naagaanizid iniwen bineshiinyan ji-ombaashinid epiichi-gashkitoonid oodi giizisong gwayak. Apii dash aanishiitamowaad, mii imaa ji-aabamisewaad ji-bi-gikendamowaad odinwewiniwaan. Nawaj igo ani-ombaashiwaad, nawaj igo ji-mino'amaazowaad gii-ikido.

The mighty eagle puffed out his chest as he strutted by the rest of the birds. He thought he would be gifted the best song, as surely no other bird could fly as high as him.

Gii-mamiikwaazo awe Migizi babaamosed gichi-inenindizod. Wiin igo gii-inenindizo ji-miinigoowizid ji-maamawi-mino'amaazod. Gaawiin awiya godag ogashkitoosiin nawaj ji-ombaashid apiich idash niin, gii-inendam.

While the Great Spirit was talking to the birds, the little hermit thrush, who was very sleepy from waking so early, wanted to take a nap. As the mighty eagle strolled past, the hermit thrush jumped onto his back and hid under his feathers. The eagle, so big and strong, never noticed the little hermit thrush tucked among his feathers.

Gii-ondami-giigido awe Manidoo Naagaanizid. Gaa-izhi-boozi-gwaashkonodawaad iniwen Migiziwan awe Miskominikesi, gii-noondengwashi aaniish. Miigwaning gii-tazhi-gaazod. Gaawiin dash ganage gii-maaminonenimigozisiin.

When the time came for the birds to earn their songs, they all flew off at once to soar as high as they could. The air was filled with thousands of birds trying to earn their songs. Eventually some of the smaller birds became tired and started to return to Mother Earth. On their downward flight, each species learned their own special song.

Mii wapii ji-bi-gikendamowaad odinwewiniwaan ingiweg bineshiinyag. Gezikaa go naa akina gii-maadaashiwag. Miziwe go naa gii-maamawibizowag ingiweg bineshiinyag. Bijiinag dash apii gii-ni-ishkibizowaad gaa-zhi-naazhibizowaad bebezhig gii-pi-miinigoowiziwaad odinwewiniwaan.

The mighty eagle, so swift and powerful in flight, was higher than all the other birds. Still, to make sure he would get the prettiest song, he continued toward the sun. He flew so high and came so close to Grandfather Sun that the tips of his feathers got burnt and turned black.

Nashke naa awe Migizi epiichi-gashki'ewizid ombaashid. Nawaj igo ishpayi'ii ogii-gashkitoon ji-ombaashid apiich idash iniwen godag. Nawaj dash ogii-misawendaan enigok ji-minwewed. Enigok gii-ombaashi awe giizisong gwayak, biinish igo ani-banzod.

The air at that height becomes thin, and eagle was getting tired and having a hard time breathing. But only after he was sure no other bird had gone as high as him did he turn around and begin his homeward flight back toward Mother Earth.

Eshkam igo ani-ombaashid awe Migizi, miish imaa gaa-ni-izhi-gaaskaaskanaamod. Apii dash dayebisewendang awe Migizi, mii imaa gaa-izhi-aabamised.

At that exact moment, the hermit thrush woke up. She could not believe how high in the air she was. She jumped off of eagle's back and started to fly upward, hoping to acquire her own song.

Upon seeing the little hermit thrush, the eagle became very angry. But he was so tired that his only choice was to continue his downward flight.

Mii imaampii gaa-izhi-goshkosed awe Miskominikesi. Gaawiin ganage ogii-debwewendanziin gaa-apiichi-ombaashinid iniwen Migiziwan. Miish imaa gaa-izhi-gabaad enigok wii-ani-akwaandaweyaashid bagosendang wiin igo ji-ondinang odinwewin.

Miish imaa Migizi gaa-izhi-dibaabamaad iniwen Miskominikesiwan, aazha gii-ni-maajiigidaazod. Gii-noondeshin dash, aazha gii-aanishiitam.

Meanwhile, the little hermit thrush, fresh from her sleep, continued to fly toward the sun. She came upon a hole in the sky and flew through it into another world. It was the most beautiful place she had ever seen. There she learned the most beautiful song.

Enigok dash gii-ni-ombaashi awe Miskominikesiins, giizisong gwayak. Miish imaa gaa-izhi-oditang iwe bagone-giizhig, gii-zhiibaased. Gii-wenda-gonaajiwan idi. Mii imaa gaa-pi-onji-gikendang ji-mino'amaazod.

Happy with the song she
had earned, she began
her long journey back to
Mother Earth.

Gaa-debisewendang
gii-ni-aabamised awe
Miskominikesiins.

On her way back down to Mother Earth, the hermit thrush thought about how the mighty eagle was probably very angry with her. Instead of joining the rest of the birds to share her song, she headed for the deepest part of the forest and sang her song only when she was sure she was far away from eagle.

Ani-aabamised awe Miskominikesiins ogii-mikwenimaan iniwen Migiziwan. Maagizhaa onishkenimigoon gii-inendam. Gaawiin ogii-misawendanziin wiin ji-wiijiiwaad iniwen godag. Indawaaj igo waasa idi megweyaak gii-ni-izhaa. Meta go apii geget bezhigoowizid ji-babaa'amaazod.

To this day, when you go deep into the forest at dusk you will hear the most beautiful melody coming from the trees. And you will know that the hermit thrush is still hiding from the mighty eagle — and singing the prettiest song of all the birds.

Mii go geyaabi ani-jekaakwa'aman, mii go geyaabi wii-noondawad ani-noondaagozid awe Miskominikesiins. Mii go geyaabi ani-gaadood epiichi-mino'amaazod.

Author's note: This story was passed down to me by my father, Terrell "TZ" Zimmerman.

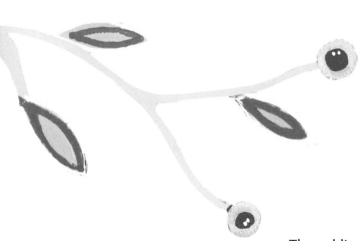

The publication of this book was supported though a generous grant from the Elmer L. and Eleanor Andersen Publications Fund.

mnhspress.org

The Minnesota Historical Society Press is a member of the Association of University Presses.

Manufactured in China.

10 9 8 7 6 5 4 3 2 1

∞ The paper used in this publication meets the minimum requirements of the American National Standard for Information Sciences—Permanence for Printed Library Materials, ANSI Z39.48-1984.

International Standard Book Number

ISBN: 978-1-68134-285-6 (hardcover)

Library of Congress Control Number: 2023950044

Learn more about the hermit thrush and hear its pretty song at AllAboutBirds.org.